DK READERS

BEGINNING
TO READ ALONE
2

The Little
Ballerina

Written by Sally Grindley

DK

A Dorling Kindersley Book

Laura pulled on her leotard
in front of her bedroom mirror.
She bent her legs and then
straightened them.
It was a perfect plié (plee-AY).

A Note to Parents and Teachers

DK READERS is a compelling reading programme for children. The programme is designed in conjunction with leading literacy experts, including Cliff Moon M.Ed., who has spent many years as a teacher and teacher educator specializing in reading. Cliff Moon has written more than 160 books for children and teachers. He is series editor to Collins Big Cat.

Beautiful illustrations and superb full-colour photographs combine with engaging, easy-to-read stories to offer a fresh approach to each subject in the series. Each DK READER is guaranteed to capture a child's interest while developing his or her reading skills, general knowledge, and love of reading.

The five levels of DK READERS are aimed at different reading abilities, enabling you to choose the books that are exactly right for your child:

Pre-level 1: Learning to read
Level 1: Beginning to read
Level 2: Beginning to read alone
Level 3: Reading alone
Level 4: Proficient readers

The "normal" age at which a child begins to read can be anywhere from three to eight years old. Adult participation through the lower levels is very helpful for providing encouragement, discussing storylines and sounding out unfamiliar words.

No matter which level you select, you can be sure that you are helping your child learn to read, then re

DK

LONDON, NEW YORK, MUNICH,
MELBOURNE, and DELHI

Created by Leapfrog Press Ltd
Project Editor Naia Bray-Moffatt
Art Editor Jane Horne

For Dorling Kindersley
Senior Editor Linda Esposito
Senior Art Editor Diane Thistlethwaite
Pre-production Francesca Wardell
Picture Researcher Liz Moore
Photographer Andy Crawford
Jacket Designer Chris Drew
Ballet Consultant Alison Good

Reading Consultant
Cliff Moon M.Ed.

Published in Great Britain by Dorling Kindersley Limited
80 Strand, London WC2R 0RL
A Penguin Company
This edition, 2013

Copyright © 1999, 2013 Dorling Kindersley Limited, London

2 4 6 8 10 9 7 5 3
002-187468-07/13

A CIP catalogue record for this book is
available from the British Library.

ISBN 978-1-40938-192-1
Colour reproduction by Colourscan, Singapore
Printed and bound in China by L Rex Printing Co., Ltd.

The publisher would like to thank the following
for their kind permission to reproduce their photographs:
Key: t=top, a=above, b=below, l=left, r=right, c=centre
Camera Press: 9br; /Andrew Crickmay: 31tr; Mary Evans
Picture Library: 5br; Royal Opera House/Catherine Ashmore: 25tr
Models: Amy Berry, Naia Bray-Moffatt, Rosie Fisher, Alison Good
Robyn Hewitt, Alex Johns, Lizzie Knight, Siobhan McCleod,
Guy and Jack Westbrook, and Olivia and Grace Williams.
In addition, Dorling Kindersley would like to thank:
Avril Mills for permission to photograph
in her ballet studio, Dance-A-Ramix.
Gill Cossey and Monica Clark
of Chameleons Face Painting, Woking.

All other images © Dorling Kindersley.
For further information see: www.dkimages.com

Discover more at
www.dk.com

"Hurry up!"
said Laura's mother.
"You don't want
to be late for
ballet school today."

French names

Ballet steps have French names because they were first written down in France more than 300 years ago. French king Louis XIV (1638–1715) danced in several ballets.

Laura opened a cupboard and took out her best ballet shoes. Today the school was putting on a show – "The Big Bad Dog and the Two Little Kittens".

Laura had a part
as a rabbit.
She couldn't
wait to dance
in her first show.

"Good luck,"
said Laura's mum
on the way
to school.

At the school, Laura looked for her best friend, Miranda. But she couldn't see her anywhere. The other children chatted happily as they put on their shoes.

"In you come,"
said their teacher, Mrs Beth.
"Straight to the barre and warm up."
Laura stood at the wooden rail.
"Where's Miranda?" she wondered.

Using the barre
Dancers hold on to
the barre, a wooden
rail, to keep steady
while they practise.

"Hold on to the barre,"
said Mrs Beth.
"Feet in first position.
And gentle pliés
in time to the music."
Then they practised the five positions.

First, Laura stood,
heels together, and
toes turned out
to the side.

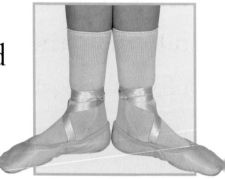

First position

Then she pushed
her feet apart
in second position

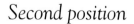

Second position

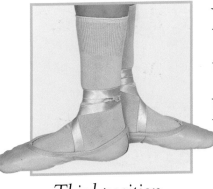

Third position

Next, she moved the heel of one foot halfway in front of her other foot.

Then she put her right foot in front of the left, a foot's length between them.

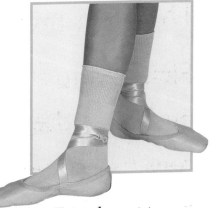

Fourth position

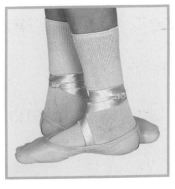

Fifth position

Finally, she slid her right foot flat against her back foot.

Laura tried hard
as she did her
steps at the barre.

Then the class
did arm movements.

"Let your head and eyes
follow the movements
of your arms,"
called out Mrs Beth.
Laura moved
her hands
lightly around
her body.

"We'll stop there," called out Mrs Beth. "Come and sit down."

Laura sat on the floor with the other dancers. "Poor Miranda has hurt her foot. She won't be able to dance today."

The children gasped.

Miranda was one of the kittens.

Who would play her part?

"I'd like you to take her place, Laura.
You have already practised
all the steps with Miranda."
Laura felt excited and scared
at the same time.
Now she had one of the main parts!

Laura's hands shook
as she put on Miranda's costume.
"Meow," said Kate, the other kitten.
"Meow," Laura giggled.
She felt a little better.

Just then Jane, the Big Bad Dog,
and Angie, the Good Witch,
came dancing in on tiptoe.
"Hooray!" everyone cheered.
Jane and Angie were the best dancers
in the school.

While the other children put on their costumes, Laura practised with Kate, Jane and Angie.

Dancing on pointe

Older dancers with strong legs and feet wear pointe shoes. With pointe shoes they can dance on the tips of their toes.

At the end of the ballet
Laura had to do an arabesque
(ar-uh-BESK).
"Try one now," said Mrs Beth.
Laura stood on one leg
with her other leg
stretched out behind.
Suddenly her ankle wobbled.

"You can do it," said Mrs Beth.
"Stare at something
straight in front of you."
Laura stared at the clock and
lifted her leg again.
This time she didn't wobble.

"Make-up time!" called Mrs Beth. She painted Kate's and Laura's faces to look like kittens.

Then she checked everyone's
costumes and make-up.
"We're ready!" said Mrs Beth.
"Walk to the hall
and wait behind the stage.
Good luck, everyone."

Laura stood in the wings
at the side of the stage.
Then the ballet began.

The Big Bad Dog
leapt across the stage
in a grand jeté (gron she-TAY).

The stage
Names are given to different parts of a stage. The wings are at either side of the stage.

Behind her came the Good Witch
and the rest of Laura's class.

Then it was Laura's turn
to go on stage.
Her heart beat faster.
"Pas de chat," (pah de SHAH)
Laura said to herself
as she and Kate jumped sideways
across the stage like cats.

In the front row
Laura's mother looked surprised.
Laura was supposed
to be a rabbit!

Laura danced the steps
she had practised.
The music helped her and
she began to feel like a kitten.
She forgot all about the audience.

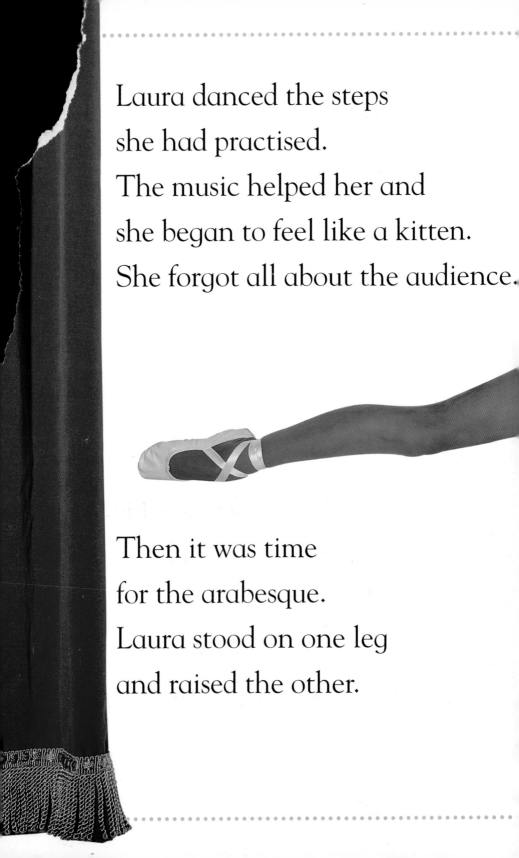

Then it was time
for the arabesque.
Laura stood on one leg
and raised the other.

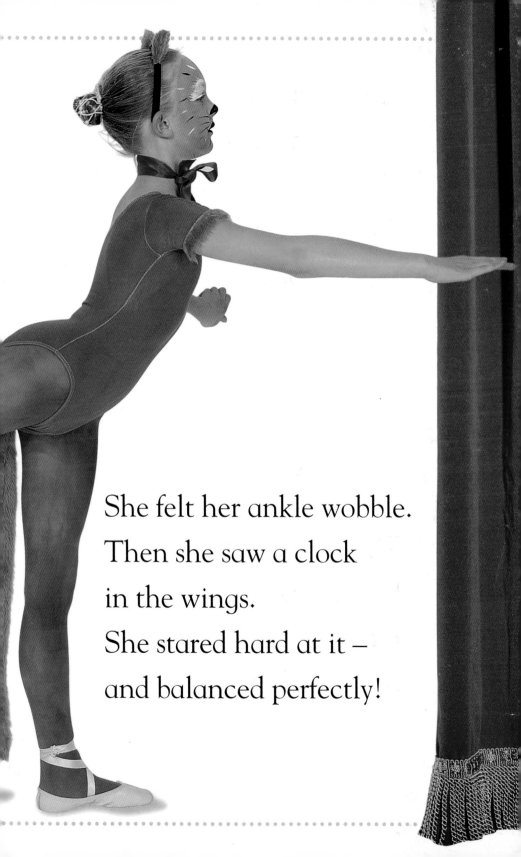

She felt her ankle wobble.
Then she saw a clock
in the wings.
She stared hard at it –
and balanced perfectly!

As the ballet ended
the audience began to clap.
Laura and the other dancers
took their bows.
Laura smiled at her mother,
who was clapping wildly.

Bow

Dancers bow to their teacher at the end of a class, or to the audience at the end of a show.

Laura thought being a ballet dancer was the best thing in the world!

Ballet steps

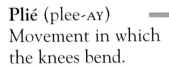

Plié (plee-AY)
Movement in which
the knees bend.

Battement-tendus
(bat-MON ton-DOO)
The foot is slid along
the floor until it points.

Grand jeté
(gron she-TAY)
A big jump from
one leg to the other,
with legs outstretched
in the air.

Pas de chat
(pah de SHAH)
Meaning
"step of the cat" –
a leap sideways.

Pirouette
(peer-uh-WET)
A dancer spins
around
on one leg.

Arabesque (ar-uh-BESK)
A dancer stands on one leg
and lifts the other straight up behind.